earring

fly

globe

house

nickel

Obo

pine cone

quilt scrap

rocket

wishbone

X-ray Vision Man

Yellow Guy

zebra

SAM SORTS

(One Hundred Favorite Things)

marthe jocelyn

TUNDRA BOOKS

For
Sam, Willa,
Joe, Deeksha,
and Rishab

Text and illustrations copyright © 2017 by Marthe Jocelyn

Tundra Books, a division of Random House of Canada Limited, a Penguin Random House Company

Library and Archives Canada Cataloguing in Publication
Jocelyn, Marthe, author, illustrator
Sam sorts / written and illustrated by Marthe Jocelyn.
Issued in print and electronic formats.
ISBN 978-1-101-91805-0 (bound).—ISBN 978-1-101-91807-4 (epub)
I. Title.
PS8569.O254S24 2017   jC813'.54   C2015-905760-4
C2015-905761-2

Published simultaneously in the United States of America by Tundra Books of Northern New York,
a division of Random House of Canada Limited, a Penguin Random House Company

Library of Congress Control Number: 2016933020

Edited by Samantha Swenson • Designed by Five Seventeen • Photography by Ian Crysler •
Digital image preparation by Rachel Topham, Five Seventeen, and Ian Crysler
The artwork in this book was rendered in paper collage • The text is set in Ashcan BB.
Printed and bound in China

www.penguinrandomhouse.ca

1 2 3 4 5   20 19 18 17 16

TUNDRA BOOKS   Penguin
Random
House

Sam's things are in a heap.
Time to tidy up.

First he finds Obo the robot, one of a kind.

Then two snarling dinosaurs,

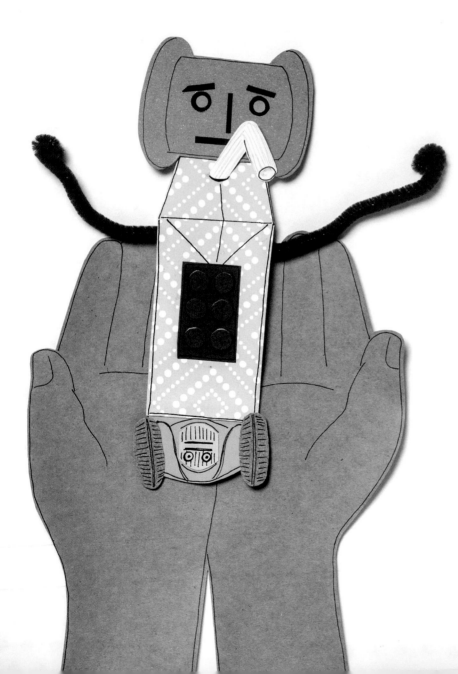

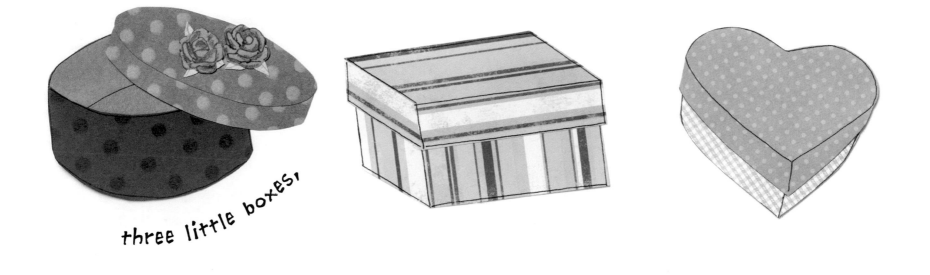

three little boxes,

and four fake foods.

How many things is that?

Sam gathers up the animals and the bugs for a parade.

So many legs! Too many to count?

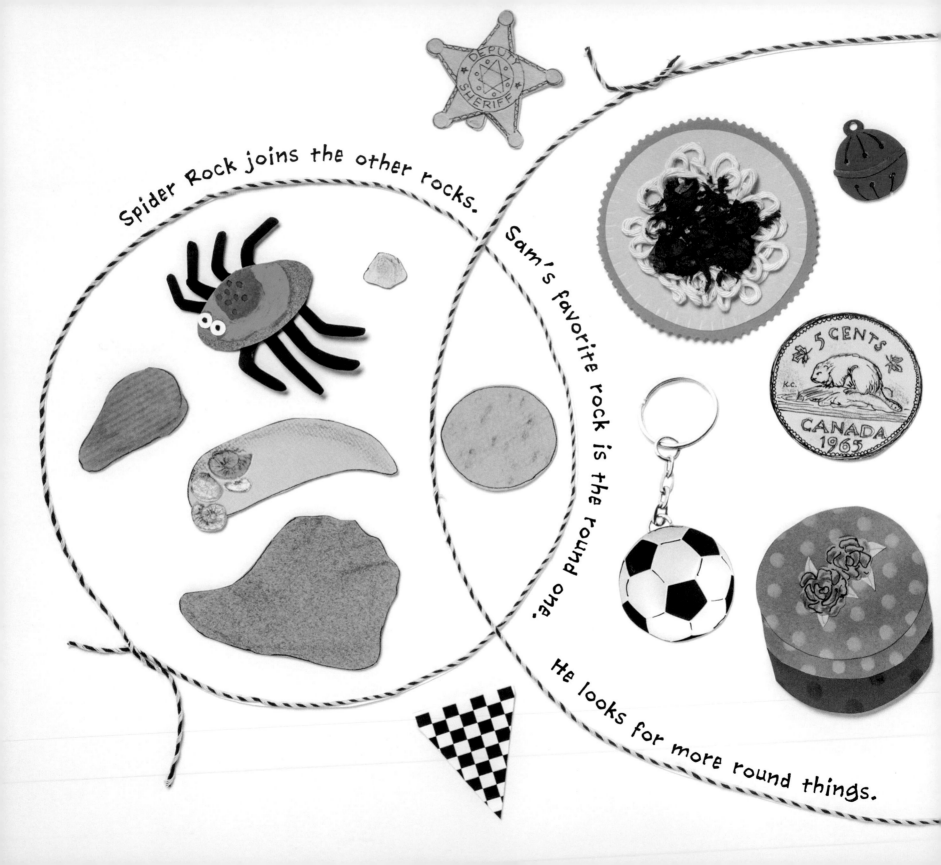

Spider Rock joins the other rocks.

Sam's favorite rock is the round one.

He looks for more round things.

Two of the buttons are exactly the same.

What else comes in twos?

Another way Sam makes a pair is by finding a rhyme.

Some things match because they have stripes.

A few have dots or holes.

Only one has checks.

The snake is striped AND green . . .

Sam has things of every color.

Sam thinks up lots of categories.
Are there other sets to add?

Soft

Fuzzy

Bumpy

Noisy

Pointy

Smelly

Sam starts a new group of things.

Tails

Things from Nature

Water from Lake Huron

Shells

Rocks

Feathers

Bones

Tree Parts

Feathers and leaves can float.

What else floats?

Things without wings that fly

Some things float and some things fly!

Things with wings that fly

Things with wings that don't fly

Sam made some of his things all by himself.

The one he likes best is Obo.

100%

But Sam has lots of other guys too.

Uh-oh. Sam's things are still in a heap.
Time to tidy up.

All sorted. How many categories? How many things?

Then Sam makes something big with all of his things . . .

...Well, all of his things except one!

alligator

banana

cowboy

dice

iguanadon

jingle-bell

knight

leaf

mustache

scissors

tooth

unicorn

valentine